This Book Belongs to:

Este libro le pertenece a:

I dedicate this book to the memory of my loving mother and to
your mother, wherever she may be. I know mine is in Heaven.
And I know she looks down lovingly and fondly on me for
telling this true story that has brought so much light and
healing to so many. I love you, Mama—DP

In memory of my grandmothers, Adeline Hines and Shirley Boynton.
And for my other grandmother, Iris Hughes, with love—BBH

Dedico este libro a la memoria de mi cariñosa madre y de todas las madres,
dondequiera que estén. Yo sé que la mía está en el cielo.
Sé que desde allí me mira con ternura y amor, feliz de que cuente esta historia
que ha llevado luz y consuelo a tantos.
Te quiero mucho, mamá —DP

A la memoria de mis abuelas, Adeline Hines y Shirley Boynton.
Y para mi otra abuela, Iris Hughes, con amor —BBH

GROSSET & DUNLAP
Penguin Young Readers Group
An Imprint of Penguin Random House LLC

Penguin supports copyright. Copyright fuels creativity, encourages diverse voices, promotes free speech, and creates a vibrant culture.
Thank you for buying an authorized edition of this book and for complying with copyright laws by not reproducing, scanning, or distributing any
part of it in any form without permission. You are supporting writers and allowing Penguin to continue to publish books for every reader.

The publisher does not have any control over and does not assume any responsibility for
author or third-party websites or their content.

"Coat of Many Colors" copyright © 1969 by Dolly Parton. Illustrations copyright © 2016 by Brooke Boynton-Hughes. All rights reserved.
Published in 2016 by Grosset & Dunlap, an imprint of Penguin Random House LLC, 345 Hudson Street, New York, New York 10014.
GROSSET & DUNLAP is a trademark of Penguin Random House LLC. Manufactured in China.

Design by Giuseppe Castellano
The art was created in pen & ink and watercolor.

Library of Congress Cataloging-in-Publication Data is available.

ISBN 9780451532374
Special Markets ISBN: 9781524789664 Not for Resale

3 5 7 9 10 8 6 4 2

This Imagination Library edition is published by Penguin Young Readers, a division
of Penguin Random House, exclusively for Dolly Parton's Imagination Library,
a not-for-profit program designed to inspire a love of reading and learning, sponsored
in part by The Dollywood Foundation. Penguin's trade editions of this work are
available wherever books are sold.

DOLLY PARTON

COAT *OF* MANY COLORS

EL ABRIGO *DE* MUCHOS COLORES

illustrated *by* Brooke Boynton-Hughes

ilustrado *por* Brooke Boynton-Hughes

traducción *de* Teresa Mlawer

Grosset & Dunlap
An Imprint of Penguin Random House

Back through the years
I go wanderin' once again,

Una vez más vuelvo la mirada,
a través de los años,

back to the seasons of my youth.

hacia los días de mi infancia.

I recall a box of rags that someone gave us,
and how my mama put the rags to use.

Recuerdo una caja de retazos que alguien nos regaló,
y el uso que mi mamá les dio.

There were rags of many colors,
but every piece was small.
And I didn't have a coat,
and it was way down in the fall.

Había retazos de muchos colores,
pero todos eran pequeños pedazos.
Yo no tenía un abrigo de invierno,
y el otoño avanzaba a grandes pasos.

Mama sewed the rags together,
sewin' every piece with love.
She made my coat of many colors
that I was so proud of.

Mamá cosió junto los retazos
y puso en ello todo su corazón.
Me hizo un abrigo de muchos colores
que me llenó de orgullo e ilusión.

As she sewed, she told a story
from the Bible she had read,

Mientras cosía, me contó una historia
que en la Biblia una vez leyó

about a coat of many colors
Joseph wore, and then she said,

sobre un abrigo de muchos colores,
que una vez José vistió.

"I hope this coat will bring you good luck and happiness."

«Que este abrigo te traiga suerte y dicha», mamá dijo.

And I just couldn't wait to wear it,
and Mama blessed it with a kiss.

Como yo quería usarlo,
con un beso lo bendijo.

My coat of many colors
that my mama made for me,
made only from rags,
but I wore it so proudly.

Mi abrigo de muchos colores
que mamá hizo para mí,
hecho solo de retazos
que con orgullo lucí.

Although we had no money,
I was rich as I could be,
in my coat of many colors
my mama made for me.

Aunque no teníamos dinero,
yo muy rica me sentí
con mi abrigo de muchos colores
que mamá hizo para mí.

So with patches on my britches
and holes in both my shoes,

Con huecos en los zapatos
y parches en mis pantalones,

in my coat of many colors,
I hurried off to school,

presurosa caminé a la escuela
en mi abrigo de muchos colores.

just to find the others laughing
and making fun of me

para encontrar a los otros niños
que se burlaban de mí

and my coat of many colors
my mama made for me.

y de mi abrigo de muchos colores
que mamá hizo para mí.

And, oh, I couldn't understand it,
for I felt I was rich.

¡Oh, yo no podía entenderlo!,
pues me sentía afortunada.

And I told them of the love
my mama sewed in every stitch.

Y les hablé del amor
que mamá cosió en cada puntada.

And I told 'em all the story
Mama told me while she sewed,

Y les conté a todos la historia
que mamá me contó aquel día,

and how my coat of many colors
was worth more than all their clothes.

y cómo mi abrigo de muchos colores
más que todas sus ropas valía.

But they didn't understand it,
and I tried to make them see
that one is only poor
only if they choose to be.

Pero ellos no lo entendieron,
y traté de hacerles ver
que uno solamente es pobre
si eso es lo que elige ser.

Now, I know we had no money,
but I was rich as I could be

Hoy sé que aun sin dinero,
yo muy rica me sentí

in my coat of many colors
my mama made for me . . .

con mi abrigo de muchos colores
que mamá hizo para mí . . .

made just for me.

solo para mí.

People ask me all the time, out of all the songs I have ever written, what is my very favorite. It's an easy answer for me, because without a doubt, "Coat of Many Colors" is the most special to me. The song, and now this book, captures so many strong feelings and emotions.

It warms my heart to know that for many people, these words have become a lesson to try to stop bullying in school. On that fateful day, I felt the terrible hurt when people made fun of me. It is a pain that takes a long, long time to go away. In fact, it never really went away until I sat down and wrote this song. Writing the song finally allowed my broken heart to heal.

There is absolutely nothing wrong with being different. I think those who choose to bully just don't know how to handle somebody different from themselves. I hope this book can plant the seeds of tolerance, understanding, and acceptance in their hearts.

And for those of you who may already have been victims of bullying, please know the hurt can heal. If this book can help but one child find comfort, then I guess all my dreams for this book will have come true.

Love always,

Dolly

P.S. I have written a special song just for you! It's called "Making Fun Ain't Funny." If you want to download this song, go to this link: imaginationlibrary.com/music.
... And it's free!

La gente siempre me pregunta que de todas las canciones que he escrito, cuál es mi preferida. La respuesta es fácil, porque, sin lugar a duda, *Coat of Many Colors* es la que tiene un significado especial para mí. La canción, y ahora este libro, encierran un sinfín de sentimientos y emociones.

Me conmueve saber que para muchas personas esas palabras han servido de lección para luchar contra el acoso escolar. Ese fatídico día, sentí un inmenso dolor cuando los otros niños se burlaron de mí. Es un dolor que tarda mucho tiempo en desaparecer. De hecho, el dolor nunca se fue hasta que me senté a escribir esta canción. Escribir la letra de esta canción hizo posible que finalmente mi corazón roto sanara.

No hay nada malo en ser diferente. Los acosadores son gente que no sabe cómo tratar a las personas que son diferentes a ellos. Espero que este libro siembre la semilla del respeto, la comprensión y la tolerancia en sus corazones.

Y para todos los que han sido víctimas de acoso, sepan que ese dolor se cura. Si este libro logra dar consuelo aunque solo sea a un niño, entonces sabré que las esperanzas que puse en él se han visto realizadas.

Con amor siempre,

Dolly

P. D.: ¡Escribí una canción especialmente para ti! Se llama *Making Fun Ain't Funny*. Si quieres descargarla, visita este enlace: imaginationlibrary.com/music.
... ¡Y es gratis!